Supermarket on Mars

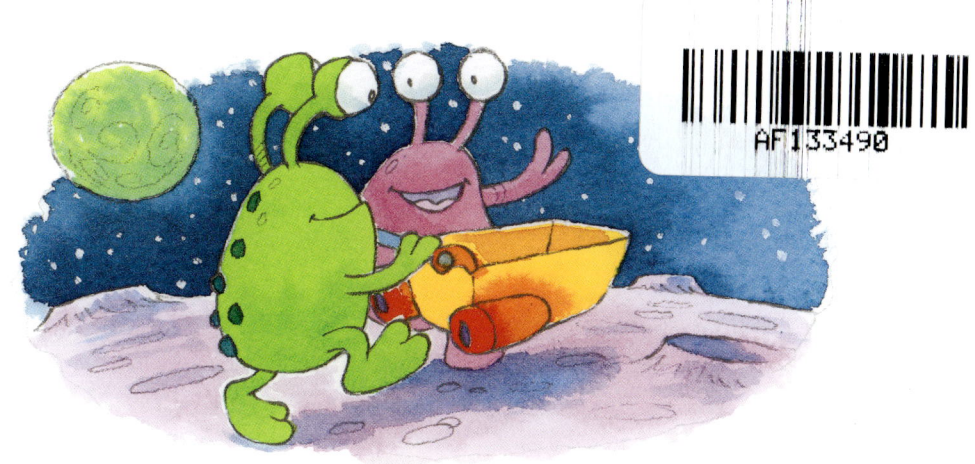

Celia Warren
Illustrated by Daniel Howarth

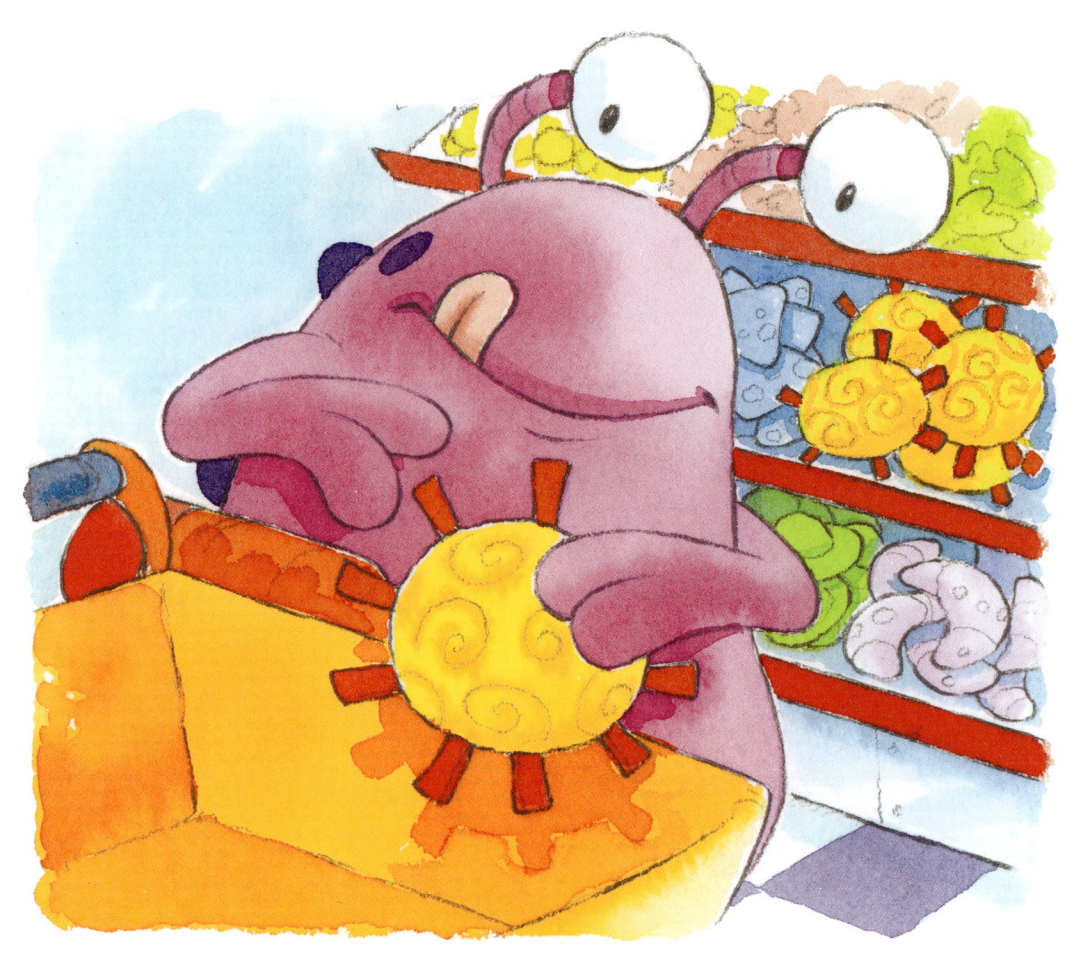

In goes a sun bun.

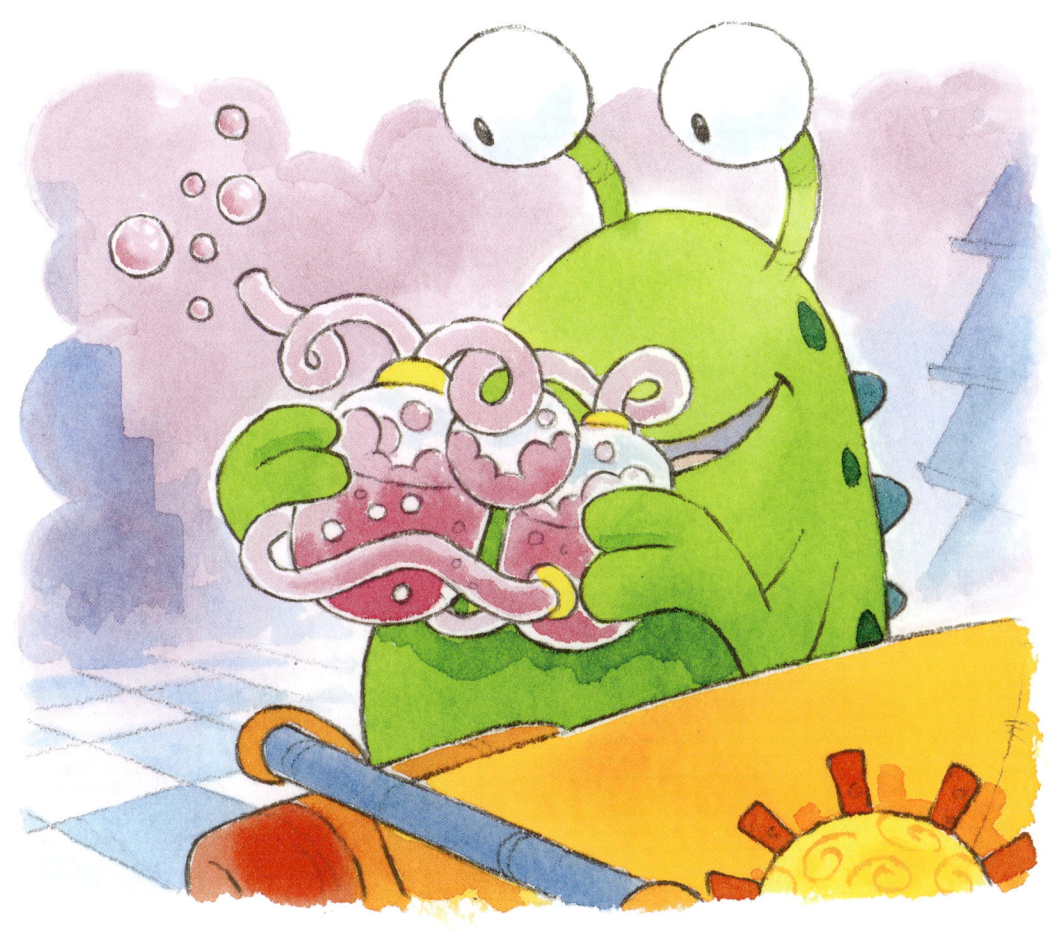

In goes a pink drink.

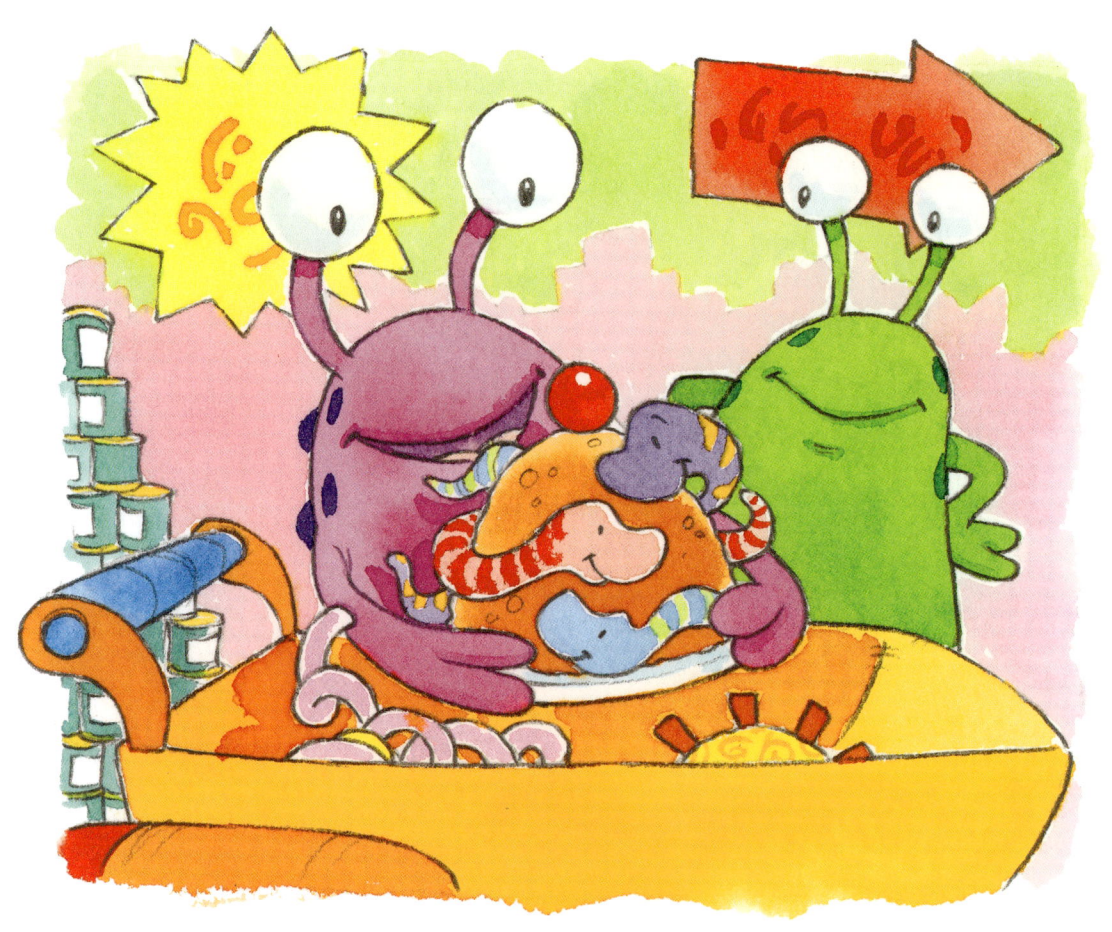

In goes a snake cake.

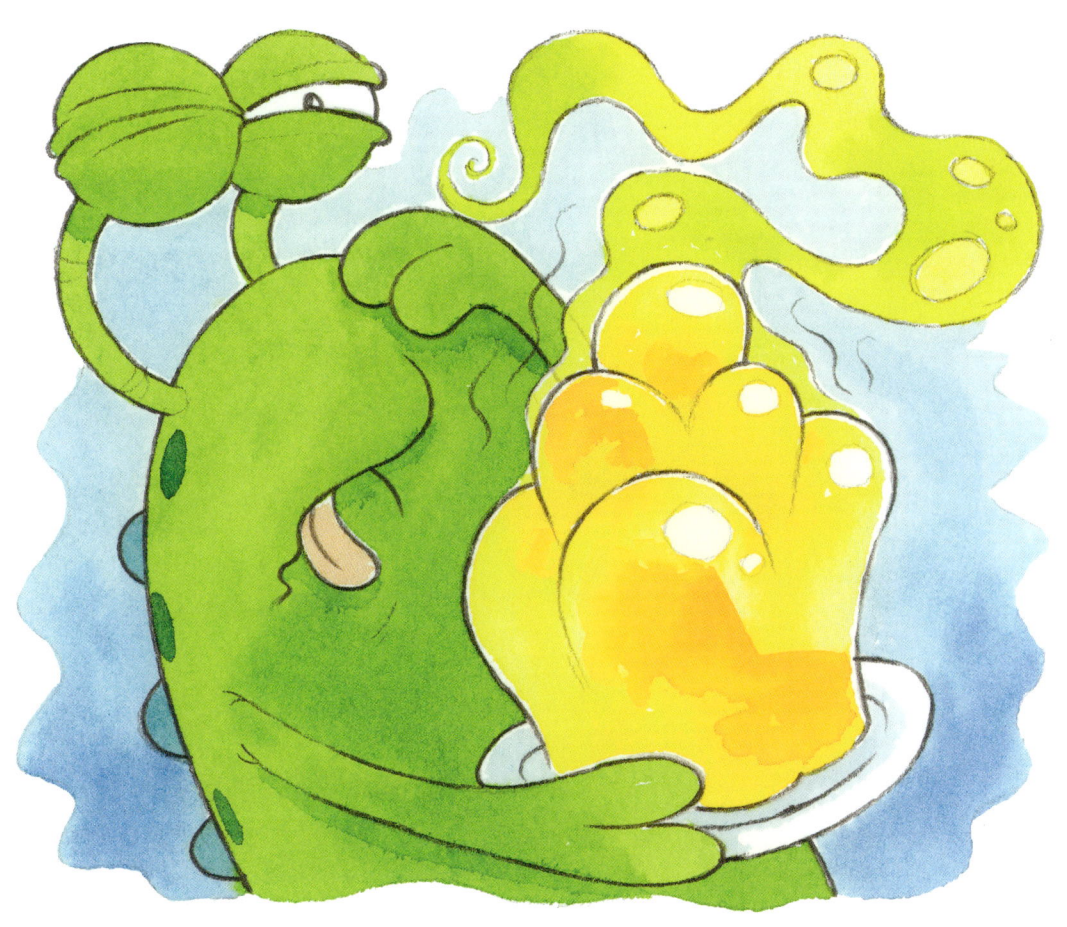

In goes a smelly jelly.

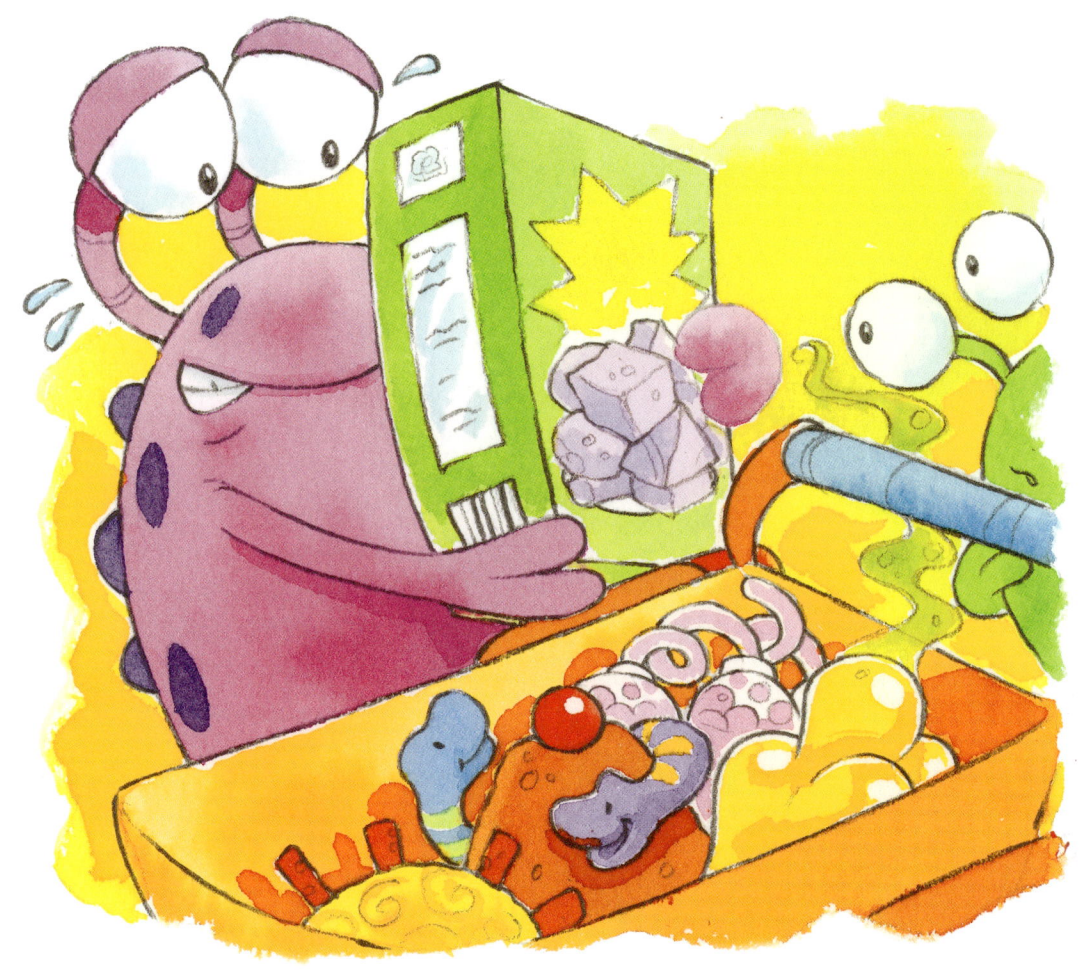

In goes a box of rocks.

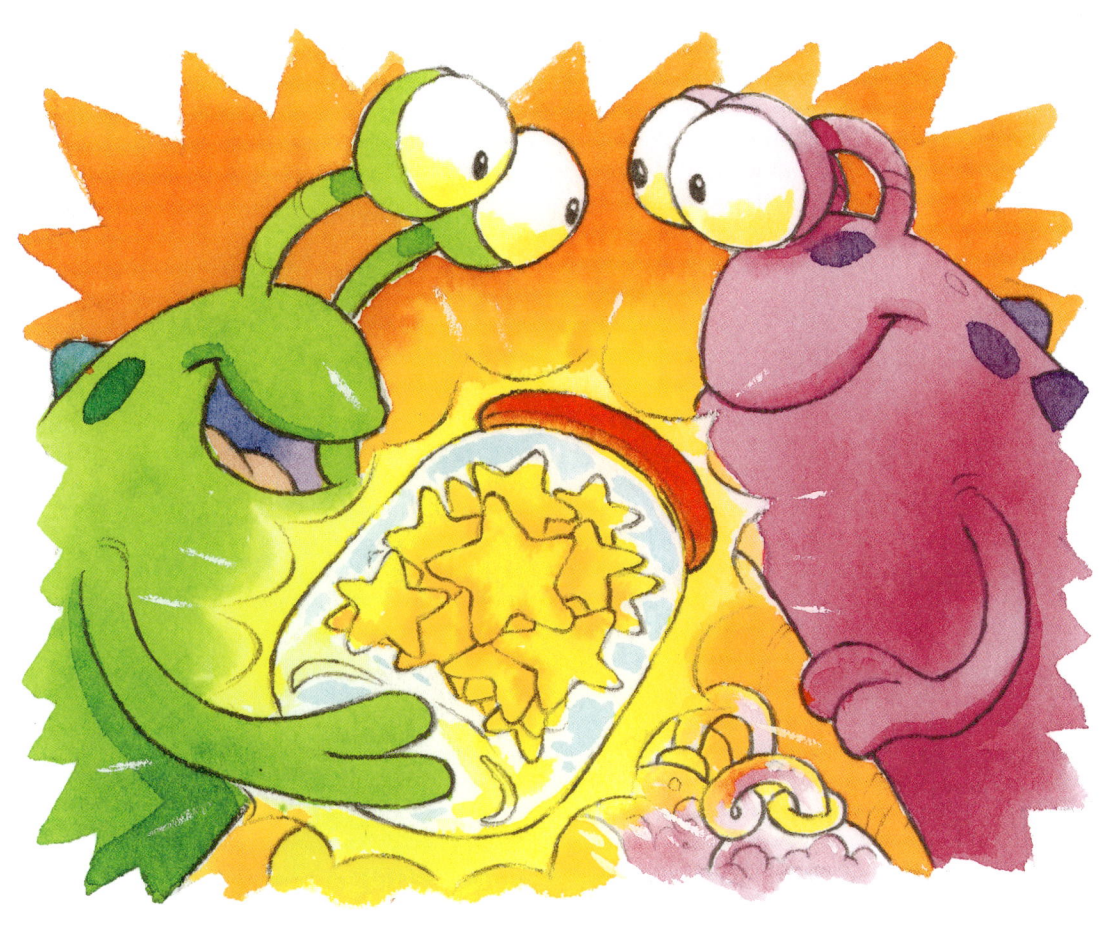

In goes a jar of stars.

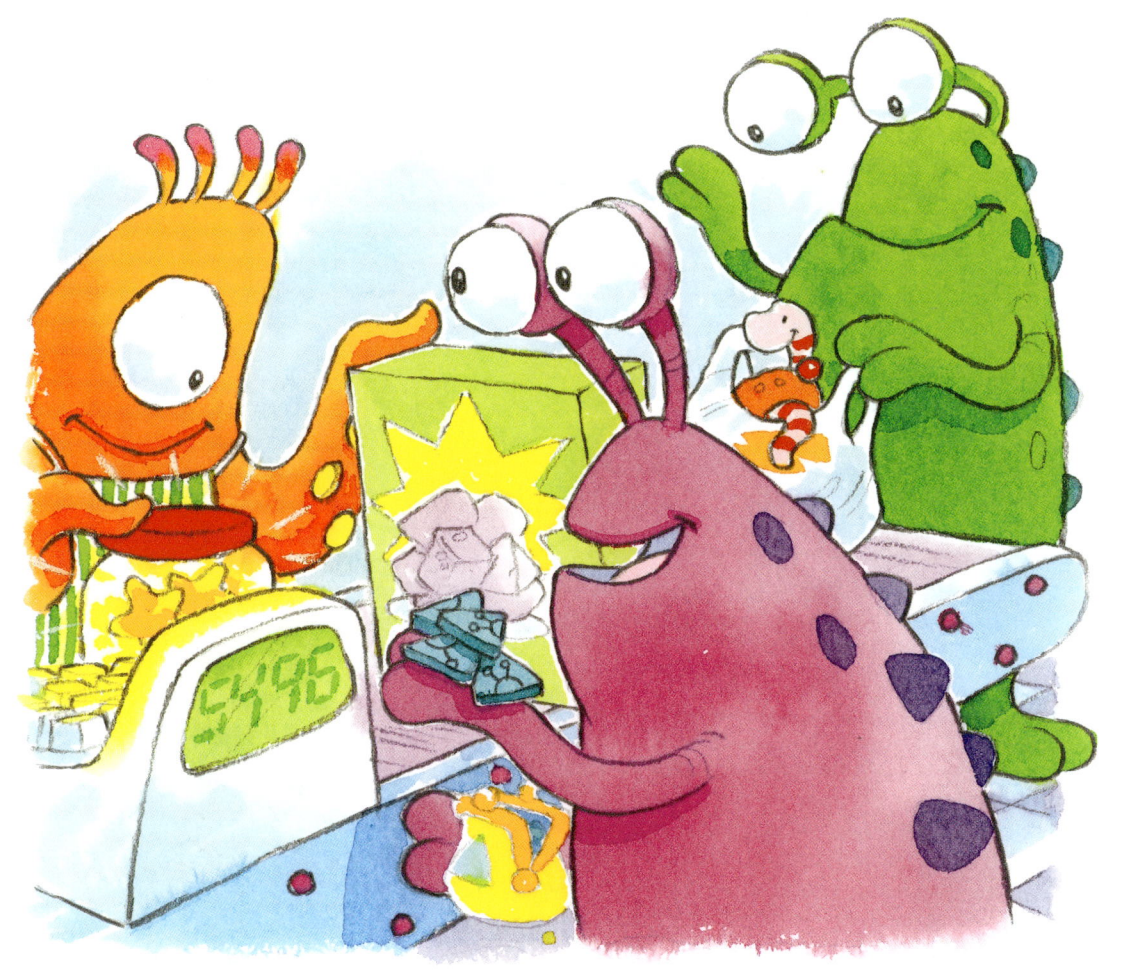

We like to shop on Mars.